The Arrangement

Vol. 7

H.M. Ward

www.SexyAwesomeBooks.com

Laree Bailey Press

COPYRIGHT

Laree Bailey Press
First Edition: August 2013
ISBN: 978-0615860787

THE ARRANGEMENT

Vol. 7

CHAPTER 1

I blink at Sean as my stomach crashes into my shoes. The way he looks at me makes the hairs on the back of my neck prickle. Goose bumps line my arms. It feels like I stepped into a freezer. I manage to choke out, "That's not true. How could it…"

Sean's dark gaze locks with mine for a moment. Every thought in my head says *run*.

On some level I knew there was something wrong with him, that Sean had this darkness hanging over him. I thought it was grief. The way that he acts screams unresolved grief over his wife's death, over losing his only child. But this, this revelation, chokes me into silence. My feet are glued to the spot.

Sean watches me for a second. It's almost like he hopes that I'll run and never look back, but I don't move. I won't. For a moment, there's no air. I'm falling through space, lost in his eyes. *Sean can't be a killer.* I think it over and over again, but the twisting inside my stomach won't stop. His words are true. I can feel the weight of his confession and it scares me. I've been fighting too hard to stay alive and this man says he snuffed out two lives before they got going.

I don't look away. It isn't that I don't believe him, it's that I see something else there. The darkness is tied to death, but this wasn't a grisly murder. I feel it in my bones, as though the premonition is part of me.

Sean finally looks away and turns. "You're not running away."

"Yeah, I'm a little crazy like that." I try to steady myself, but I can't. My pulse is pounding in my ears and my body is tense, ready to run. I try to sound calm. "Do you want to tell me what happened?"

Sean glances over his shoulder at me, on his way to the bar on the other side of the hotel room. He stops. The way his eyes crinkle in the corners gives him away. It's a brief squint, like pain crawling up from deep within and trying to consume him. Sean swallows it back down. "Are you sure you want to know?" His voice is steady, cold, and utterly detached.

It feels like the icy hands of a ghost that's walked up behind me are touching my shoulders. I suck in air and step toward him. "Tell me."

Sean didn't expect that answer. I can see it in his eyes. He turns away from me and heads toward the bar. After pouring a drink, he reaches for his laptop. The screen flickers to life. He taps the keys and clicks before turning it toward me. "Read."

I glance down at the headline from one of the country's largest newspapers—SEAN FERRO ACCUSED OF MURDERING WIFE AND UNBORN CHILD. I reach for the computer and scan the article, but I don't see what I'm looking for. It's more of what Gabe told me about Sean appearing cold and detached, about how he didn't look grief-stricken. The article ends with a link to a follow up story. I click through the articles one by one, watching pictures of Sean age like years are passing rather than months. I feel his gaze on the side of my face, but I don't look up. I lean against the bar and set the computer down. I click through to another article. I stare at his picture, at the words and accusations, and swallow hard.

I click the final link to the last story. FERRO AQUITTED. My heart is racing, slamming into my chest. I feel sick. I try to clear away all the emotions and think. I don't understand how they didn't find him guilty. The paper made it sound like it was an open and shut case. Sean Ferro brutally killed his wife in a jealous rage. He left her on their bed, bleeding to death, and went to work. When he returned home that night, he called the police. All the papers said the 911 call was a hoax and that his wife had died hours before he returned home that night. There were no other suspects.

When I finish reading, I glance up at him. Sean's gaze meets mine and fear twists inside of me. Have I misjudged him so badly that I can't tell a messed up guy from a sociopath? Did he really do this? Sean doesn't show emotion, but that doesn't mean anything. Neither do I—well, not in front of people I don't trust. I had that stone-cold look on my face when they lowered my parents into the ground. I remember people saying that it wasn't right for me not to cry, but I didn't. Not then. They didn't see my tears or hear my sobs. Sean's the same way. I know he is, so lack of emotion doesn't mean what the papers say it means.

"This isn't true." I push down the laptop screen and keep my gaze locked with Sean's. It's a statement, a fact. There's information missing from the papers, of course. But there are also things that Sean never shared about this. I see the secrets burning in his eyes.

His eyebrow twitches. Sean shakes his head and looks down. Dark hair falls into his eyes. "You're naïve, Avery."

"You're hiding something, Sean. You'd rather let people think you killed your wife than tell the truth?"

Sean stares at me. My words seem to grip him in a way that makes him anxious. I'm too close, and he can't bear it. "The truth is there in black and white. I killed her. I'm a jealous man. Everyone knows that. I know you've heard I have a tempter, that I can be more than persuasive when things don't go my way." He steps toward me, brushing his chest into mine. I swallow hard, but don't back away. "When are you going to get it through your head that I'm not the guy you think I am?"

"You're exactly who I think you are. You're cowering behind this…" I'm yelling, waiving my hands around as I speak. "This manifestation of lies."

He laughs. The dark, rich, sound sends a chill down my spine. "Yeah, keep telling yourself that."

"Tell me the truth."

"The truth was printed."

"This is only part of the story. Omissions are lies."

Sean's eyebrows lift. "You're going to pull philosophical crap on me now? Unbelievable. Accept me for what I am and stop looking for things that aren't there." Sean shakes his head like he's annoyed and slams his glass down on the counter. When he breathes, his back expands. His shoulders are so tense. Sean's fingers are turning white as he grips the granite countertop. He rounds on me with his lips pressed tightly together. "I'm not your savior, Avery. There's no knight, no horse, no happy ending—not with me. That shit isn't real."

"I never said I wanted the white knight."

"It's written all over your face."

Damn it. The thought is nice. I mean, who hasn't dreamed about being rescued when their life turns to shit. It's the epitome of every fairytale out there—the desire to be saved—but I learned the truth a long time ago. I bristle. My fingers ball at my sides. This subject is beyond striking a nerve with me, because I live it, I live the life where no one comes and the heroine is left utterly alone.

"Fine," I bite back, admitting it, "but you only got half of it right. I believe in white knights, but the only knight in this story is me. No one saved me. I've fallen so far that I can't even see the way out anymore. I'm at the bottom of Hell and I found you.

"You're lost, broken, and completely fucked up. You're not like me, but you want to be. The difference between us is that I still have hope and you lost yours a long time ago." I swallow hard, wondering how crazy I am for saying this. "I'm not leaving no matter what you tell me happened to Amanda. At the very least, I'm your friend. I'm not the one who's going to walk away here."

His blue eyes are so narrow, but for a split second, they widen. Sean blinks and the look of shock is gone. He steps closer to me, closing the space between us. "Do you have a death wish?"

Sean's irritating me more than anything else. His response, the absolute refusal to talk about what happened to his wife tells me so much, but I still don't know what happened. I make an aggravated sound in the back of my throat and say, "Stop asking stupid questions. Spill your guts or let's get on with things." *Stupid, stupid, stupid.* Where did that come from? Did I seriously say that?

Sean doesn't conceal his surprise this time. Wide-eyed, he steps back and looks me over once. "Are you serious? You still trust me? What the hell is wrong with you?"

"Me? What's wrong with me? Are you seriously asking that question, you messed up bastard?" I slam my palms into his chest and shove, but he barely moves. "You're such a goddamn hypocrite, and you can't even tell."

Sean grabs my wrists and holds on tight. His breath washes over my face when he exhales. "Enlighten me, Miss Smith."

I glare at him for a moment and then spit it out. "You're telling me to run away, that there's nothing worth saving—that you have nothing left to give—but then you have the nerve to go and say you care about me.

"I can't come back from where I've gone. People don't recover from things like this. I know that. You know that, so don't patronize me with your fake empathy, because that's what it is if you feel nothing, if you're as hollow as I am, if —"

Before I can take another breath, Sean's mouth comes crashing down on mine, cutting off my flow of words. Sean pulls me against his chest and tangles his fingers in my hair, pulling hard. The kiss is demanding and all consuming. He doesn't want me to talk. I'm saying things that he doesn't want to hear. I'm gasping between his lips, kissing him back, wondering how far I'm willing to go. There's no coming back from this side of Hell. I know his agony; he knows mine.

I know there's more to his wife's death than Sean's telling me, that he's hiding something bigger and using the murder accusations to mask it. I feel it in my gut. There were pictures of Amanda Ferro in there, smiling next to a serious Sean. In one picture, his arm was around her with one hand protectively on her stomach as she stepped off a curb. Sean cared about her and the baby. He wanted them. I know he can't live with his loss. I see it on his face and hear it in his voice every time he speaks.

Fathomless pain courses through his veins to the point that he's gone numb.

I understand. I wanted to be where he is and feel nothing anymore, but this—the fact that hookers can do things that bring Sean back—means something. Sean doesn't want to stay in the depths of that torment anymore, but like me, he can't find the way out. Too much time has passed. Too many scars are still raw and refuse to heal. It brings out the desperation, the maddening need to cling to life even when there's nothing to hold on to anymore.

There's a darker version of Sean that I've never seen. If I allow things to continue, if I stay here with him, I'll stand face to face and see the horror replay before his eyes, like he's lost in a nightmare that never ends. I want to free him from that so badly, but no one can save Sean, not when he's like this. Not even me.

Sean's kisses become more demanding. He pushes me back against the bar and lifts me onto the counter. His hands are forceful when they slide over my thighs, pushing my dress up to my hips. He steps between my legs and dips his head to my lips again. I tangle my fingers in his hair. Heat spreads across my skin, trailing in a wake behind Sean's hands as they move over my body. He palms the curve of my ass, holding me tightly in his hand as his kisses grow hotter and hotter. His tongue is over my lips and in my mouth as his lips crush into mine.

Ragged breaths escape from him like he can't slow down, even if he wanted to. I reach for Sean's shirt and unbutton the top enough to slide my hands inside. When I move to touch his shoulders and dip my hands down his chest, Sean jerks back. He grabs my wrists and slams them into the wall. I gasp, half turned on, half frightened.

Sapphire eyes, dark as night, bore into me. Sean doesn't blink. It's like he forgot himself for a moment. The tension in his jaw fades after a second, and he leans in and presses his lips to my throat while pinning me to the wall. I let him. I let him hold me there even though every ounce of my being wants to fight to break free. I hate feeling trapped and the way he holds me and presses against my neck makes me feel like I can't move.

Normally, I would fight back, but I don't. I tilt my head back and close my eyes, allowing the fear and lust to course through me in unrelenting waves. I suck in a jagged breath and Sean pushes against me harder. I wonder if he's doing it on purpose, if this is part of what he wanted. I want Sean, all of him, on any terms that I can get him.

The hot kisses stop and I notice how incredibly intoxicated I feel. My eyes flicker open and I look at Sean. He's still leaning into me, still holding my wrists to the wall. His voice is raspy, all air and heat. "When it's your turn, you won't hold back?"

CHAPTER 2

His question surprises me. I can hear the strain in Sean's voice, like the idea of being with me on my terms scares the hell out of him. I nod, looking into his eyes. "I'm taking what I want from you. I expect you to do the same. No holding back."

Sean is frozen. For a moment he doesn't move. I wonder what he wants to do, how far he wants things to go. Anxiety flashes across his face and is gone. Sean nods once and releases my hands. They fall to my sides, aching. The place he held me burns and my underarms ache.

Sean scoops me off the counter and carries me to the bed. Fear starts trickling through me. At first it's small and manageable. I swallow it back down and it turns into nervous excitement.

Sean places me on the bed. I'm on my back, looking up at his beautiful face. I'm scared. I don't know if I can do this, but I want to. There's a wall between us and I want it to come crashing down. No, it's more than that. I want to be everything Sean needs.

"Are you sure you want to do this?" Sean asks. My throat is so tight that I can barely swallow. I nod. Sean looks away and runs his hands through his hair. He sighs, like he hoped I'd say no. Sean stands there, staring at me, lost in thought.

I push up on my elbows. "Do you need this?" His eyes are locked with mine. Sean nods. The expression on his face is timid and so unlike him, but there's something in the depths of his eyes that says he needs this like he needs air. Without it, he'll lose what's left of himself.

I watch Sean for a moment. I want to be the one he needs, the one he trusts with everything. I could back away and he'd let me. I could let him continue doing these acts with nameless faces, but I can't do that to him. He needs me and I need him just as much. My decision solidifies. "Then, I want to be the one to give it to you. Will it work, since you know me?" I wondered about that part. It tripped Sean up when he first ordered me. He said it wouldn't be the same.

"I think I figured something out. But, there's no way out, Avery. Once we start—"

I cut him off. "I'm not leaving."

Sean breaks my gaze and nods. His throat is tight. He swallows hard. "Roll over." I do as he says. Sean grabs my ankles and pulls me back over the edge of the bed so my legs are on the floor. He spreads my ankles and ties each one to the bedpost. I try not to think about it, but panic is building inside of me. The other strap is worse. Sean leans hard on my back, knocking the air out of my lungs as he ties my wrists. Within seconds I'm bound to the bed, facedown, and can't move. My heart beats faster. I can't control it, but I try. I take a slow breath in and let it out.

Sean sets a video camera on the dresser. It turns on and the red light blinks, telling me it's recording. I don't like it. That freaks me out as much as being tied down. "What are you doing?"

"You're going to watch it later."

I laugh, like that's most ridiculous thing I've ever heard. "No, I'm not."

"You will. You'll beg me to see it." Sean's gaze is so dark, so intense. Fear is crushing into me.

My voice quivers. "No, I won't."

He smiles and sits next to my head. "Last chance, Smitty."

"I'm not leaving, Jones."

Sean touches my cheek gently. "All right. I'll see you when this is over." He pulls a blindfold from his pocket. My heart explodes in my chest when he ties it over my eyes and the world goes black. It makes the claustrophobia worse. Sean knew it would. I hear his voice, but it sounds far away. My pulse pounds harder. Sean is gentle this time. I wonder how long it'll stay this way. His voice is closer when it finally registers. "Open your mouth."

I do as he asks, not sure what to expect. Nerves flutter through my stomach, making me queasy. My mind is screaming at me, telling me that I'm going to die. I try to ignore my bonds, but it feels like they're searing into my skin. There's no way to forget that I'm tied down, even if I attempt to ignore it. I breathe through my mouth when I feel the gag slip between my lips. He tugs it hard and the smooth fabric gets forced to the back of my mouth. Sean ties it tightly. The amount of fabric in my mouth makes it feel like there's no air, like I can't breathe.

Panic surges through me, stronger this time. Mentally, I know I can breathe, but I feel like I can't. My wrists twitch, making the straps pull tighter. I can't slow my heartbeat. I can't picture a meadow and mentally escape to somewhere else. Sean took every fear I have and rolled them together. I can't calm down. Anxiety races through me in an avalanche. I try to thrash and pull away, but the only thing I can move is my head.

Sean's voice comes from behind me. He says something that I can't make out when I feel my skirt lift. His hands cup my ass and he feels my smooth skin before pressing his hips against my butt. "Calm down or you'll hyperventilate. You can breathe, Avery. Slow down. Focus on my touch, on my hands."

Fear is strangling me. I try to stop, I try to do what Sean says. The roaring in my ears makes it so much worse. I hate being confined. *You're trapped. You're trapped. You're trapped.* The words have been on repeat since he tied me down. I didn't even realize what I was thinking until I tried to focus on his touch. The words ring hollowly in my mind as I try to focus on Sean's hands. One is on each side of my thigh, sliding slowly up the outside of my leg. He must be kneeling next to me because I can feel his breath on my legs. Sean rubs his hands up and down, one finger at a time. I gain control of my breathing again. The panic recedes. The only thing I can feel is the cold fear that's frozen in my stomach and Sean's hot touch on my bottom.

Something cold touches my hip and I wince. Sean drags its point over my hip, gently scraping my skin. It's sharp, but he doesn't cut me. The threat is there, the fact that I'm at his mercy isn't lost on me. I don't trust anyone, but somehow I volunteered to be tied to Sean's bed and let him do this to me.

He loves me. The metal bites into my skin slightly and is gone.

"Breathe," Sean commands. His hand is on my back, waiting for me to do it. Slowly, I inhale and let the air fill my lungs. I let it out slowly and do it again. "Good girl."

Sean's hand is gone. I try to focus on breathing and forget about everything else, but it's hard. I want to rip my arms out of the restraints. Nervous energy lines my arms and legs. It's pouring into my stomach like a tidal wave. I forget what will happen and pull my arms. The tug tightens all four restraints. I whimper into the gag and blink frantically behind the blindfold.

For a moment, I freak-out thinking that Sean left me tied to the bed alone, but then

I feel his hand on my hip. He slides his palm over my bare skin and loops his thumbs around my panty. I hear a metallic snip, then another, and the little scrap of fabric is gone. I'm so tense that I don't know what I want. I should have asked how long this would take. I thought I could do it, but now I don't know. My pulse pounds harder, faster. I can barely breathe. My tongue is shoving the gag, trying to make more room in my mouth.

Warm palms slowly inch up the V of my legs. At first I can barely feel Sean's touch, but as he gets closer to the top of my thighs, I squirm. My hips jerk to the side, but I don't fall. I'm still in my heels, with my dress fanned around me, pulled up, exposing me.

I have no idea what's going to happen next, but suddenly everything takes a turn. Sean's hand lands hard on my bottom, stinging the skin. The unexpected hit makes me yelp into the gag. My hands ball into fists, but I can't move. I'm not used to being hit. I don't like it. My instinct is to hit back, but I can't. Before I have time to think, Sean's elbow is on my back. The air is forced out of my lungs at the same time his hand grips my pussy. He finds me quickly and forces his fingers inside. I'm dry, not ready for him. Sean thrusts another finger inside, stretching me. He pushes in and out fast, over and over again while I struggle to breathe.

It's the worst thing he could have done. It feels like I'm on fire inside and out. My mind is screaming to fight him off, but I can't move. Sean slips in another finger and pushes inside of me, thrusting deeper every time. His elbow lightens and I suck in a sharp breath, but as soon as I do it, Sean knocks the wind out of me again. His fingers move faster between my legs, making my body respond. Damp heat covers his fingers making them slick. He pushes into me up to his knuckles as I fight for air. Holding his hand there for a moment, he leans hard on my back. I fight for breath and then suddenly, he pulls out and I can breathe.

For a moment, the only thing I can hear is my breath. Then the door opens. Horror washes over me. Someone's here. Sean is speaking softly and I can make out another voice. What is he doing? I hope the other man goes away, but he doesn't.

Sean says, "This will only be a minute."

Another voice says, "That's more than fair."

Fear consumes me. He's going to share me and I can't move. I can't do a damn thing. I thrash my head on the bed, trying to get the blindfold off. I scream into the gag and shake my head. I know I said I'd do anything, but I never dreamed he'd do this.

Before I can think, there's a hand on my bottom and I hear a zipper open. Panic rises up within me. It's not Sean. Sean is standing in front of me. I hear his voice whispering in my ear to keep breathing. *But, I can't. I can't. I can't.*

Fear twists inside of me, turning to something else. I want to kill him. Before I have time to think, I feel the man's hard length on my backside. He leans into me, pushing in deep. He sighs and stays still for a moment before he starts rocking. He pushes into me over and over again, each time thrusting deeper. My hands clutch at the bed, and I grit my teeth, trying to bear it, when something presses hard on my back.

It's heavy, like a suitcase. It makes it harder for me to breathe. The guy thrusts harder, more wildly. His hands grip my ass. He rides me until I'm so sore that I can't stand. My knees start to give out. He pulls out after he comes and walks across the room. I hear the sound of his shoes, his voice.

"She's tight," he says.

I hear Sean agree, and he takes the thing off my back. "Very."

They talk, but I'm not listening. I'm planning on ripping Sean's face off as soon as he unties me. A hand slaps my cheek and pulls me out of my thoughts. "Breathe."

My jaw is aching. I'm biting the gag as hard as I can. I must be holding my breath because my lungs feel like they're on fire. I pull at the restraints, ignoring Sean's warnings, pulling myself tighter and tighter. My legs spread wider, and my face is getting smashed in the mattress, but I don't stop yanking. I can't. I have to break free. *I have to. I have to.*

Sean's voice moves through the room until he's behind me. His fingers push inside and linger. "Push into my hand." I don't move. He withdraws his hand. For a moment, nothing happens, then his hand spanks me hard. "Do it." Sean pushes into me again and I push back.

I can't breathe. I can't move. I can't do this.

My body is covered in sweat. My wrists ache. I'm an incoherent ball of rage and fear. And lust. I don't understand the last part. I don't understand why I'm wet or why I want Sean to touch me at all. It makes no sense, but my body responds to him. I can't help it. I push back into his hands, feeling him inside of me and I want more.

Sean touches me again, stroking me, making me moan. I can't focus for long. I feel the bonds biting at me. My mind flashes to images of me trapped in a coffin, stuck beneath layers of dirt. I can't move. There's no air. I claw at the box, but I'm trapped.

Fear consumes me, swallowing me whole. I thrash again, or try to, but there's no slack left. My nails claw at the bed. I can't stand it. Sean's voice is in my ear, but I don't listen. I scream into the gag, but I know this isn't over. This is what he wanted—me completely out of control. It's what Sean was waiting for. As my mind snaps, Sean rubs his dick across my butt. He presses against the wrong spot and I'm so scared that he's going to try and fuck my ass. I wait for it. He pushes against me harder this time, but at the last second he moves. His hips slam into mine and I feel his erection sink into me. Sean's fingers tangle in my hair. He pulls hard, yanking my head back as he fucks me. I feel like an animal. There's no love in Sean's actions, no man in the monster. He rides me until he shudders and fills me with come.

My heart is racing, ready to burst. I feel used, cheated, and completely crazy. He broke me. I can't think. My mind won't process anything. Slowly, thoughts reemerge through the haze. There was another man. My mind swirls around that thought for a moment. I feel sharper, like I'm waking up. The blind panic is clearing. Inviting another guy in was not part of the plan. I don't even know who he was. I breathe in slowly, ticking off the minutes on my fingers, waiting for Sean to untie me—but he doesn't.

The bed next to me dips and I hear his voice in my ear. "Lots of women fantasize about being with two men, but that thought scares you. Not seeing his face, not knowing his name. It's too much." Sean's finger touches my cheek and I jump. He withdraws his hand. "But you needed too much. You keep your mind so carefully under control and I needed it."

The blindfold unties and I can see him. Sean is shirtless. His pants hang low around his hips. He's lying on his side next to me, watching me. He reaches for me, brushing the hair away from my eyes. I'm pulling on the restraints as hard as I can. I want to scream at him but he doesn't ungag me.

"Fear is like love. It has the same depths, the same intensity." He's watching me, running his finger along my cheek. He's concerned that he pushed me too far too fast. Sean continues, "So does pain. You use pain the way I use fear—to forget." Sean looks at me for a moment and then pushes off the bed.

The ties on my ankles come free first and then my wrists. Before Sean has time to look up, I fly at him, ripping the gag away as I go. I slam into him hard, knocking Sean backward. He hits the floor. Before he has time to blink, I'm on him. My knee is over his throat, but I don't press down.

I'm so mad, so angry, that spots are blinking bright red and white, glittering like Christmas lights. "What the fuck gives you the right to invite someone else in here! I said I was giving myself to you! YOU!" I want to hurt him, I want to, but I can't. I wait too long. Sean sees the chance and takes it. He reaches behind me and knocks me down. Sean rolls on top of me, pinning me to the floor with his entire body.

"It's what I wanted." He's so calm, so fucking calm.

I scream and try to claw him, but Sean grabs each hand and slams it to the floor. He leans in close to me. "I want you so broken that you can't trust yourself. I want you to give all of yourself to me."

"You said you loved me! How could you share me?" I'm still fighting him, trying to break free. "How could you—" His lips come crashing down on mine before I can get the question out. Sean kisses me, but I don't kiss him back. I suck his lip into my mouth and bite down.

Sean pulls away, and a bead of blood drips off his lip and onto my face. It rolls down my cheek. Sean won't let me up. "I do love you. I love everything about you. I can't believe you bit me." He blinks at me several times, like I'm the weird one. I thrash under him and almost break free, but he lays on top of me, completely stilling me. "Avery, there was no one else."

The roaring in my ears is so loud. I don't think I heard him right. "What?"

"This is where you ask to see the video." Sean watches me, waiting for rationality to return, but it doesn't. He explains, "I won't share you. I won't ever share you. It was part of what I wanted—you, completely vulnerable to anything and everything I could possibly want—so I made you think there was another person here, but there wasn't." Sean stops for a second and watches the information sink into my brain. "I didn't think you were a two guy kind of girl." I shake my head, staring at him, wondering if it could possibly be true. My eyes flick to the nightstand—to the video camera. "Do you want to watch it?"

No. But I have to. The bastard. He planned this. The whole thing. My jaw is hanging open. I don't understand him. I don't know why he'd make me think that. I'm so mad. I should have known, but there was no way to know—not this. He's so twisted. I growl, "That was a mind fuck. That's what you wanted—body, mind, and soul. All of me."

"Yes," he nods, slowly admitting it. "I want all of you, in every way. I want to own you. I want you to plead with me, to crawl to me on your hands and knees and beg me to take you. I want you to surrender to me, to my wants, and give me anything and everything."

"You don't want me to give you anything. You want to take it."

"Perhaps." I give him a look. "Fine, you're right. It's not the same if there's no fight. I want to break you down and make you mine. Doing this let me fuck with you in every way possible, and god, I want that more than anything." He leans down and presses a light kiss to my lips.

When he sits up, Sean lets go of my wrists. "Watch the video with me. I want you to." Sean stands and offers his hand. I take it and he pulls me to my feet. His hands slip around my waist until he finds the zipper. He pulls it down and my new dress falls to the floor. I'm standing in front of him wearing a little black bra. He reaches around and undoes the clasp. Sean takes the bra off me and tosses it on the floor. I'm naked. His eyes sweep over me, before pulling me to the couch on the other side of the room. Sean pulls me onto his lap and plays the video. His hands wander while we watch, and I can't hide how turned on I am. What the hell is wrong with me? Sean doesn't say much. He just watches me, taking in my reaction.

I watch his hips buck into mine on the TV as he fucks me. I thought he was someone else, but there isn't anyone. There's a recorder by my head. I didn't see it before. Sean must have moved placed it there after he blindfolded me. My stomach twists. I watch the video and squirm. The fear is palpable. I never thought I'd do anything like this. Watching it after the fact just seems wrong, but I can't look away.

I blurt out, "I wish I could see your face." I wonder what his eyes look like as he does that to me. I wonder how much of him is there when he's like that. His body is beautiful, covered in a sheen of sweat. His muscles tense and release as he pushes into me. I watch him thrust over and over again. His head hangs back as he looks up at the ceiling when he comes. The tension rolls out of his back and he relaxes before pulling out of me.

God that turned me on. I'm already sore, but my body doesn't seem to care. Sean watches me through the entire video. After it's over, I glance at him. I don't know what to say. He's messed up, but so I am because I'm so aroused. I want him so much.

Sean inches his hand further up my leg. I part them for him and lean back against his chest. I close my eyes when he touches me down there. Sean rubs gently, making lust swirl deep inside me. I want to turn around and straddle him. A smile creeps across my face when I realize something— it's my turn.

CHAPTER 3

I'm still trembling, still on edge from what he did to me. I glance over at Sean in his jeans and bare feet. He changed at some point and ditched the suit from earlier. I don't see it on the floor. My gaze flicks up to his chest and those perfectly lickable abs. I can do anything I want. That was our trade. I hold out my hand to him and he takes it. I pull Sean up from the couch and he follows me across the room.

Sean stops walking. It makes my arm jerk and I stop and look at him. He's tense, like I'm going to hurt him. "Can you tell me what we're going to do? At least clue me in a little bit?"

I smile softly at him and shake my head. Dark hair falls over my shoulders. I'm naked and standing on rose petals in front of the bathroom door. A sliver of light shines through the dark room. "I won't hurt you."

"I know, it's just…" Sean runs his fingers through his hair and then down his neck. He stretches, showing off that ripped body. "I'm not good at these things."

"Are you backing out of your end of the arrangement, Mr. Jones?"

Sean grins at me every time I call him that. It conjures memories of the first night I met him. "No, of course not, but—"

"Then, don't worry about it. Trust me a little, okay." I'm cautious with him. For some reason, Sean seems brittle, like he'll crack in my hands if I'm not careful. I don't want to break him. I don't want him in more pain than he already is, but I think this will help.

I start talking about things—my papers, Mel, grad school—as we wait for the tub to fill. I have my hands on his skin, keeping the contact between us. Sean looks leery, but doesn't shy away. When I turn off the water, I turn back to him. I reach for his waist and slip the button through the hole on his jeans. They loosen. I tug him toward me and look into his eyes. "It's all or nothing, Ferro."

"I'm not going anywhere, Stanz." He leans in and presses his lips to my temple. The kiss is so gentle, so uncertain. It makes me melt. There's a softer side that Sean keeps hidden. The one time I saw it was the first time we were together. Maybe it was an accident, but tonight I'm not asking for accidents. I'm asking for all of him.

Looking down, I lower the zipper on his pants slowly. I slip the clothing off his long, lean legs and toss them across the room. Taking his hands, we both step into the tub. Sean sits down and looks up at me. I hesitate before sitting down across from him, which was not my original plan.

Sean notices. "What's the matter?"

I smile softly. "Nothing, just tired I guess."

"You said you wouldn't lie to me, Smitty." Sean takes my ankle and pulls my foot to his lap. He rubs little circles on the bottom of my heel.

"I don't want to say it. It seems greedy and I have enough."

"Say it."

"This hardly seems fair. I don't know every nook and cranny of your mind, but you think I should just let you into mine." I'm defensive. I don't want to share everything, not if he isn't.

Sean grins. "I already know what's bothering you, I just want to hear you say it."

I laugh. There's no way he knows. "Yeah? Then tell me. What do you already know?"

Sean looks up from under dark lashes. His eyes slip over my face and trail down my neck to where my breasts disappear below the water. When his gaze returns to meet mine, he says, "You don't want to take it from me. You want me to let you in and make love to you softly and slowly. You want the piece of me that no one has access to. You want me to just let you in and give you everything you want."

I look away. My heart pounds. Sean read my thoughts perfectly, not missing a thing. It's what I was thinking, nearly word for word. It scares me—he scares me. I want to sink below the surface of the water and ask him to leave.

Sean tugs my ankle, harder this time. My butt slips and I have to grab the sides of the tub before I go under. The movement makes me forgot for a second and I look at him. He says, "You're wrong about that, you know. That piece is already gone."

"No, it's not." My voice is a whisper. It feels like I'm sinking and the sea is freezing. I'm drowning again.

"It is. I keep trying to tell you that. It's a wonder that I don't turn to ash when you touch me. I'm barely breathing, barely alive. I don't deserve you, but here you are offering everything. I'd give it to you, Avery, but—"

I don't want to hear it anymore. Sean doesn't seem to know. If his heart was gone, completely destroyed the way he thinks, then this wouldn't bother him at all. It would be boring or an inconvenience, but that's not it. Intimacy scares him.

I shift in the tub and crawl toward him. Sean stops talking. I place a hand on his shoulder and wrap my legs around his waist before lowering myself onto his lap. Sean's shoulders are so hard, so tense. His hands find my waist. His touch is gentle.

When I look up into his eyes, I say, "Breathe."

Sean nods and takes a long slow breath. His chest swells under my fingers. I won't push him too far, too fast. I know that sitting face to face like this is hard for him. I'm guessing it reminds him of his wife. Maybe it's something they used to do and I'm conjuring ghosts. I don't know. I just know that he's still in there somewhere, and the way Sean's eyes flicker to life when we're like this is impossible to miss.

I trail my fingers along his shoulders before taking the soap. I rub it between my palms and press my hand to his shoulders gently. I rub in slow circles, leaving a trail of suds as I move down his body with my hands. When I finish, I give him the soap and he does the same to me, carefully washing me with gentle touches. My eyes close for a second when Sean rubs his hands over my breasts, under, and around the sides. The touch is good, soft, but firm. I feel him harden beneath me as he does it.

My eyes flick open. Sean is watching me, lips parted, breathing a little too hard. I lean forward and press a kiss to his lips. Sean's hands slip out of the water and up my back, feeling the curves of my body. I lean forward, moving my hips as I kiss him. When I settle on his lap again, he's hard.

Sean shifts me in his lap so we line up perfectly, and then pushes inside of me. It feels completely different than before, when he had me tied up. That felt frantic, but this makes me feel high, like a happy buzz, but so much more. Sean's hands move down my back and grip my butt. He rocks me gently making the water slosh in the tub. His eyes are locked on mine. It feels so good and my body wants the release so bad, but I don't give in to the sensations. Instead, I unwrap myself from him.

Sean seems surprised. "Avery?"

I stand and offer my hand. Sean takes it and stands. Water rolls off his beautiful body in sheets, cascading back into the tub. I take him in my arms and pull him against me. Sean wraps his arms around me and holds on tight. We stand there like that. I'm afraid to let go, but Sean makes it so I don't have to. He sweeps me up into his arms. "I wish I could save you. It's not that I don't want to…"

"I know what you mean."

Our eyes lock and the world stops. For a moment it seems like everything is fine, that it'll all work out. Maybe I am naïve, because even thinking something like that is insane.

I tell Sean where to take us. He walks out of the bathroom and to the bed. I'm still damp, so when he sets me down the sheets stick to my skin. I pat the spot next to me. Sean lies down. We're nose to nose. I thread my fingers in his hair and play with the curls at the nape of his neck.

We're quiet for a while, then Sean speaks. His voice is so soft, barely there. "You amaze me, Avery Stanz."

I smile, sleepily. "Likewise, Sean Ferro. It seems that we're opposites, doesn't it? I mean, you like things one hundred percent backwards from the way I like them—when it comes to sex anyway."

He smirks. "It's probably with other things, too. You didn't turn to stone. I did. We're so different—"

"And so alike."

Sean presses his forehead to mine. "I love you, Avery." He takes me in his arms, cradling me, and I fall asleep.

When I dream, the sea is still. It doesn't overcome me or pull me under. There's a ray of sunshine piercing through the vast gray sky and I finally feel some peace.

CHAPTER 4

Peeling my eyes open, I try to focus. I glance around and feel like someone is watching me. I blink, trying to chase away the sleepiness.

Two blue eyes are locked on mine. "Hey, lover," Sean says as he strokes the back of his hand along my cheek. Sean looks like he's been awake for a while.

I smile sleepily at him. "Don't call me that." It feels too intimate. I suppose it's true, in a factual kind of way, but he bought me. It's not the same.

"Then what should I call you?" His fingers tickle my cheek.

"I really like spray-start car girl. That was my favorite."

"It's quite a mouthful to say in bed." Sean grins. "Something shorter, perhaps? Kitten?" I cringe and make a face. "Sexy?"

"That might stick. Keep working on it." Sean's chest is bare. He's propped up on his side with his elbow. His head rests on his hand. It makes the muscles on his chest look so perfect. I want to touch him, and glide my fingers over each and every dip and hard curve. I want to learn his body, but I hesitate. I don't want to ruin whatever we have.

Sean notices me staring at his chest. "Some girls would be offended by that."

My eyes flick up to his face. "What?"

"My eyes are up here," he kids.

I laugh. "You're such a—"

"A what? I know you like what you see. I'm just calling it like I see it."

I give him a weird look. It's like he channeled Mel. "You're so—"

"So incredibly captivated by you. Yes, I am." He smiles warmly at me and resumes tracing the soft curves of my face. First his finger trails over my chin and then up my cheek. It makes my stomach dip. I love his touch. I'll never get enough of him. "It's still your turn, by the way."

"It is?" He nods. "But, I fell asleep and it's a new day."

"So, it doesn't change things. You had more in mind, and I realize that. Today is yours. We do anything you want. Tonight is mine." Sean leans in and kisses the side of my face gently. It makes me want to squeal. My mind starts to drift though and soon I'm reliving what he did to me last night. I don't know if I can do that again, and I doubt he wants to do the same thing. "What's going on in that mind of yours? I know that look. Tell me, Avery."

I glance over at him and shake my head. "Nothing." I lie, and I'm a terrible liar. I glance away from him and twirl the sheet between my fingers.

Sean scoots closer to me. He presses his naked body to the side of mine. When I look up into his face I can't breathe. "Tell me, spray-start car girl."

That makes me laugh. Sean knows how to pull my heartstrings. I wonder if he's playing me, because he could. It would be easy for him. The way he hones in on what makes me tick, and then manipulates it—he could be my best friend or my worst enemy. It scares me; he scares me. I'm quiet too long.

"A secret for a secret?" he prompts. This surprises me. I glance up at him and can tell he's serious.

Maybe he is playing me. It's way too easy for him to fish the thoughts out of my head, but I can't pass this up and he knows it. "All right. Ask me again."

"What are you thinking about?"

I swallow the lump in my throat. Glancing down at the sheet in my hands, I say, "Last night when we did things your way—it was nearly beyond me. I mean, I don't know if I could do that again." Sean is quiet. I feel his gaze on the side of my face, but he doesn't say anything. "I wish I could just give you what you want. I would, you know." I look up at him from under my lashes.

"I know," he breathes, "But it's not something to give. It's something to be taken. I'm not sure you understand what it is or what it means to me that you'd offer yourself that way... that you stayed with me." Sean reaches for my hand and presses it against his chest. I feel his heart start racing beneath my palm. The longer my hand is there, the faster it races. "This is what you do to me. Can you feel it? You know what that means, right?"

No. I'm not sure. His skin is so warm, so smooth, but the frantic beating of his heart feels wrong. I look into his face and see it. Everything he's been trying to hide, how much I scare him, how much he wants to run away from me and never come back. But something holds him here. Sean doesn't want to leave. His heart feels like it's going to explode under my hand.

I lower my gaze to his chest and lift my palm, leaving only a finger. "You're afraid of me."

Sean's quiet. He doesn't counter my words. Instead he stares at my finger. His heart continues to race like he's running from a rabid bear. I don't know what to do. My pulse picks up and pounds harder. I swallow hard and lean in to press my lips to his heart. Sean stiffens, like I'm going to stab him. I stop right before my lips touch his skin. I breathe for a moment and decide that I can't do this to him, not yet. These things will come on their own, given enough time.

But there is no time. We have today, and then I go to Henry. After that Black will hire me out to someone else. I feel so torn. Indecision freezes me in place. That's when Sean reaches for me. He slips his fingers over the side of my face and to the back of my neck. He makes the decision for me by pulling me forward that last breath. My mouth touches his skin. Sean's body stiffens like I'm hurting him, but his hand stays on my neck encouraging me to kiss him the way I want.

I want to kiss his chest over his heart, so I do it. My lips brush against his skin, once, twice, and then I press harder. My lips part and flick my tongue against him, as I press my lips to his chest. I stay there for a moment, lingering, wanting more when I pull away. I glance up at Sean. He's breathing so hard, so ragged.

A question pops up in my mind and I can't chase it away. I have to ask him, I have to know. "Why are we doing this?" My question surprises him. "It seems like we're torturing each other."

"It won't be that way forever."

"It won't?"

He shakes his head. "We'll acclimate to one another, given enough time. We might even learn to enjoy it. Will there be more time, Avery? You're still here, next to me. Have you decided to stay?"

I want to throw my arms around him and say yes, but I can't. It's not that I don't love him, I do. It's Black. It's walking away from the ability to support myself. I won't get that chance back. If things don't work out with Sean, I'll have nothing. Besides, I can't take money from him like that. My broken brain is okay with being paid for sex, but getting money just because I'm his girlfriend seems wrong.

I hedge. "That's two secrets and I haven't even gotten one yet."

He grins, "Ask away."

I want to know what happened to his wife. I want to know why he's so dark and tormented. I want to know that piece of him so badly, but I can't ask that question. I can't take that from him. Sean has to give it. I glance past him and see the sunrise streaking the gray sky. Little bits of glitter float gently by the window and I smile. A different question pops up in my mind. "What's your favorite thing to do in the snow?"

Sean blinks like he heard me wrong. Laughing, he asks, "What?"

"You heard me, Ferro. Ice skating, skiing, sledding, or what?"

"Sorry, I expected you to ask something else." He smiles the sweetest crooked smile I've ever seen. It makes a dimple appear on his cheek. I resist the urge to lick it and wait for his answer. "Sledding, I suppose."

"We can do anything I want, right?" He nods. "Then I want to take you sledding. I want to do something that makes you laugh. I want to see this quirky little grin on your lips all day. I want to go down Cardiac Hill with you, and a snowman on a toboggan.

What do you say, Jones? Are you up for it?" As I speak, I push up on the bed. By the time I'm done, I'm kneeling and practically jumping up and down. I can see the city after I sit up. The snow stuck. That means Long Island should be a blanket of white. I'm so giddy and excited that I don't remember I'm naked.

Sean's gaze devours me as I do my little happy dance on my knees. "Hell, Smitty. I'll do anything you want, but if you keep bouncing around like that, I'm going to have my way with you first."

I freeze. My jaw drops open and I laugh. My hands cover my breasts and I turn bright read.

Sean closes his eyes and smiles hard. "You did not just do that. Now, I have to have you." He pushes up to his knees and moves toward me. Taking me in his arms, Sean presses his hard body against mine. "Make love to me, Avery. Please. Don't make me wait until tonight."

Giddy glee bursts across my face, and then I do as he asks.

CHAPTER 5

Sean lets me linger in the shower. I'm sore, but in a good way. It makes me smile. I rinse off, step out of the shower, and towel off. I rub a brush through my hair as I blast the hell out of it with the blow dryer, and then pull it back into a high pony tail. I brought an overnight bag since Sean ordered me for two days. I dig around and pull out a pair of threadbare jeans, thick socks, and an oversized sweater. I'm so snuggly. Miss Black would have a stroke if she knew what I was wearing. It's completely wrong for a call girl of my caliber, but screw that. Besides, she isn't here and I doubt the other call girls take their clients sledding. I need to call her and get permission to leave the hotel as soon as I'm ready to go.

When I walk out of the bathroom I'm hit with the scent of bacon and coffee. I glance around like a starving dog, following my nose to the other side of the bed. There's a tray with silver covers over various dishes. I glance around, wondering where Sean went as I peek under a tray and steal a slice of bacon.

A cold breeze brushes my cheek, making me turn. The balcony doors are open a crack. I walk over slowly. Sean is standing outside, phone in hand, talking to someone. I smile at his back. I can't wait to wrap my arms around him and go down that crazy hill on the sled. I plan on laughing like a maniac—and let's face it—I'll probably fall off the sled a few times too.

As I walk toward the door, Sean's voice becomes clearer. "No, I won't. You're on your own, Pete. I have enough problems.

Deal with it yourself." He's quiet for a moment. Sean bows his head and rubs his temples. Whoever he's talking to is stressing him out really bad. The little vein on the side of his head is throbbing. I wonder who it is or what they want. Sean never lets anyone get to him about anything. Even when he was at the table with Henry, Sean was so cool and collected. I had no idea how jealous he was until later.

I know I shouldn't listen, that I should back away, but I can't. This seems personal and Sean plays his cards close to his chest. I want this glimpse of him. I need it. I step closer.

Sean shakes his head and pulls his coat closed. Snowflakes stick to his dark hair and the shoulders of the jacket. "You're making a mistake. Stop laughing, dickwad, and I have every right to say it. I know, all right. You don't want anything to do with that shit and if you get caught—well, I've been there. I'm not helping you. If you want it, you'll have to take it from me." Sean shakes his head, annoyed, and ends the call.

When he turns he sees me through the glass. "Avery." His voice is strained, like he's afraid of what I heard.

I push the doors open and lean on the doorjamb. A cold gust of wind hits me in the face. Folding my arms over my chest, I ask, "Who's Pete?"

"No one important." Sean's eyes dart past me toward our breakfast. "Did you eat?"

"No, not yet." I stare at him. *Liar.* Pete is someone very important. It's written all over his face. "You can tell me stuff, you know. I won't share your secrets. It's actually part of what makes this whole arrangement less call-girlish and more normal. You know, you tell me something that bothers you and I tell you something that irks me."

Sean doesn't blink. He doesn't look away or make excuses. Flurries continue to fall from the sky while the two of us have a staring contest like a pair of five year olds. Sean finally smiles and looks away. "Fine, I'll tell you, but let's go inside. I can hear your stomach growling from here."

Horror washes over my face. My tummy's been grumbling since I smelled the food. I didn't think he could hear, not with the street noise. Sean laughs and puts his arm over my shoulder as he pulls me inside. "You're so cute, so absolutely adorable. You're also a terrible snoop." He turns me in front of him and kisses the tip of my nose. Then, he swats my bottom, pushing me toward the food while he closes the doors and shucks his coat. Sean's already dressed. He's wearing a form-fitting blue sweater with a pair of jeans and biker boots.

"I wasn't snooping. You ordered food and then weren't around. It's not like I'd eat it without you." Sean glances at me and raises an eyebrow when he lifts the cover off the bacon. The nice neat stack isn't so neat anymore. "Okay, I ate that."

"I see." Sean laughs and pulls me over to the couch. He dishes up a plate and grabs himself some coffee. Sean sits down next to me and grabs a piece of bacon off my plate. As he eats, he talks. "That was my brother. He wanted to see me. I told him no."

"Why?" I'm shocked. I didn't expect Sean to tell me anything. I remember him saying something about a sibling, but Sean never talks about him. "I mean, what's so bad about seeing him?"

"If I see him, I'll cave. You might think I'm a calloused ass—"

"Your ass is not calloused." I wink at him, and clink my coffee mug to his.

Sean smiles again. It's such a great thing, making that man smile. "I'm glad you noticed." He winks at me, and then the pensive look returns to his face. "What do you think I should do?"

Holy shit. He's really asking me for advice? I freeze with my cup to my lips. I lower it and ask, "Is this a trick?"

"What?" he laughs.

"It just seems like a huge coincidence, that's all. I ask you about personal stuff, you don't tell me, so you make something up. It fits with your type of cray-cray, so why not?"

Sean presses his lips together really hard. His shoulders start to shake as he tries not to laugh, but he does a horrible job. "My type of crazy?"

"Cray cray," I correct. "Crazy-ass to the second power. Completely bat shit crazy. Cray cray."

"Yeah, I'm not saying that—like ever." Sean starts laughing again.

I roll my eyes and sip my coffee like I'm an adult. "It seemed like a logical question."

"Logic left this conversation a while ago." Sean wipes a tear from the corner of his eye. I can see old laugh lines on his face. He must have been happy at one point. The fine lines around the corners of his eyes and mouth are ghostly reminders of the man he used to be. I wonder if he's still in there. Sometimes I feel so lost, like I'm so far gone that I'll never be happy again. Then things like this happen, and Sean is laughing more than I would have thought possible.

"Shut up, Cray cray, and tell me about your brother." I bump his shoulder with mine, and finish up the food on my plate.

"Pete fell off the face of the earth a while back, severed all contact. He was going through some stuff. I got it, so I didn't try to find him. Sometimes you have to work things out on your own. I get that. Anyway, he wanted to come see me. He's asking about stuff he shouldn't be asking about. I don't want him to do what he's thinking about doing. It'll fuck him over."

"What does he want?"

"The gun." Sean's eyes glaze over. He's lost in a memory.

A gun? The hairs on my arms prickle like a bad omen. I want what's best for Sean and he's too isolated. At the same time… it's his brother. "Won't he get one from someone else if you don't help him?"

"Maybe." Sean looks over at me. "You think I should see him?"

I nod. "Yeah, I do. He needs you. Maybe he doesn't actually want a gun— maybe he just wants your help."

Sean considers what I've said. When he looks back up at me, he asks, "Come with me. Make sure I don't give it to him."

I nod. Part of me wonders why Sean has a gun and why his brother doesn't just get another one. Why try to get it from Sean? I don't know much about his family, just that Sean is estranged from them. Talking to his brother is a big deal. I hope I'm encouraging the right thing. I just think that he shouldn't be alone anymore. Living life that way is too damn hard.

Questions swirl in my mind, about Sean and his family. "Sean?"

"Yeah, baby?" He's lost in thought. Sean rubs his hands over his face and looks over at me.

"Will you ever be able to tell me what happened?" I don't say the rest. I can't seem to get the words out. He didn't kill them, there's no way. Our eyes lock and the pain that I stirred up is visible in his eyes. I want to hold him in my arms and take it all away. I have no idea what those blue eyes have seen, what they've lived through, but he's not the monster he thinks he is—he's just not.

Sean breaks the gaze and looks away. After a moment, he says, "Someday, Avery. Just, not now. This was supposed to be your day. I have one day to win you over and pull you away from Black. I feel like I'm wasting it."

"You're not wasting it." I put my hand on his knee and lean into him. Sean drapes his arm over my back and pulls me in close.

"The gun has something to do with her death, doesn't it?"

Sean nods. It's barely noticeable. "I haven't said a word about any of it to anyone. Talking about that is like shoving splinters into my eyes. I can't stand it. It drags up everything I'm trying so hard to forget. My life ended that night. I didn't care what they wanted to do to me." He blinks and stares straight ahead when his eyes reopen. "There was so much blood. People don't make mistakes like that…"

I squeeze his arm to silence him. I feel how fragile he is, like a piece of frayed rope with only a few strands left. Sean leans into me and I wrap my arms around him. Sean lets me. He doesn't tense up as soon as I touch him. Not this time. After a moment, he pulls away and stands.

"Where are you going?" I ask.

"I'm inviting Pete to dinner."

CHAPTER 6

"No," Miss Black's voice is firm. I called to tell her that we're leaving the hotel for a while. "I forbid it, Avery. If you leave, Gabe will make you wish you hadn't."

"So, I'm stuck here until Sunday morning?"

"Yes, that was written in your contract. It was explicit. Mr. Ferro has possession of you until that time. You are to do as he asks with the stipulation that you remain at the same location. I can't have you traipsing all over New York and still protect you. How would I do that?"

"Have Gabe drive us." I offer. Sean is watching me as I talk to Black. He grimaces like that was a terrible idea.

"No, stay at the hotel with Mr. Ferro. This conversation is over." She's mad. I seem to have a knack for pissing her off. The line goes dead before I can say another word.

"She hung up on me!"

Sean walks over and slides his hands around my waist. He leans in and kisses my neck. "We could go back to bed."

"No, not yet. This is important Sean." I clutch my temples, trying to ward off the headache that's growing behind my eyes. It's important because it frees him, I know it will. It's the only connection that I can make. Sean acts like himself when he forgets, when he does things that he hasn't done before. Sledding takes him back to before he was married, before his life turned to shit. I want to give him that, I want it so badly that I can't imagine staying in this room all day, tormenting him with my touches. I want to scream.

Sean takes my wrists and pulls my hands away from my face. "I'll take care of it. You go call down for extra blankets and a couple thermoses of hot cocoa."

"But—"

"Do it," he commands and swats my butt as he pushes me away.

"She isn't going to listen to you either." I sulk and walk to the phone next to the couch. Sean gives me a wicked grin before stepping out onto the balcony. He's out there forever. When he steps back inside, he brushes the snow off his shoulders and smiles at me.

"Done. Grab your coat and let's go." As he walks toward the door, Sean strips off the damp sweater. I lean forward, staring at his chest. He smiles at me before pulling on another one—black this time. "Glad you like it."

I do. He's pure yummy when he's half naked and smiling like he owns the world. For the life of me, I can't figure out how he got Black to agree. She sounded like she wanted to bite my head off. "How'd you—?"

Sean pushes me toward the door. "Money talks, Avery. I hired that thug that drives you around, too. He'll be here in a few minutes with sleds. I have to say this is the weirdest arrangement I've ever made. I just hired a guy to kick my ass if I get too handsy with you. Do I dock his pay if he takes too long to punch me? Or should I just aggravate the hell out of him the whole time?"

"Gabe hates you. That's a really bad plan."

Sean kisses my temple and adds, "Everyone hates me, babe. You're a delightful exception."

CHAPTER 7

Sean makes Gabe buy me a coat while we wait in the car. Every time I see the old guy's eyes in the mirror, shame washes across my face. Gabe thinks I'm an idiot. He watches me sitting next to Sean and he sees right through me. Gabe knows how smitten I am with Sean. Gabe has a natural grimace etched onto his face. I think he might shoot Sean just for the hell of it.

Gabe parks the car and look over at Sean, like he shouldn't leave us alone. "I'll be fine," I tell him.

Sean cuts me off, "She'll be frozen if you don't get her that coat."

"Don't steal my car," Gabe mutters.

"I could buy a fleet of these, old man. You worries are for naught." Sean grins at Gabe, and then gets the door slammed in his face.

"Well, isn't he delightful?"

"For naught? Who do you think you are, Mr. Darcy?" The corner of my mouth twitches. I shake my head and look out the window.

"I heard you like surly men."

"I like men who don't piss off Gabe. I like men who keep their beautiful heads on their strapping shoulders."

"You think he could take me?" Sean look surprised. Gabe is a brute, but Sean is younger.

"I think Gabe could whack you and toss you in the trunk, yeah. So stop trying to piss him off. The only reason he went inside is because he's been yelling at me to wear a coat, too."

"Awh, he likes you! Old man Gabe has a crush on my girl." Sean smiles broadly.

I roll my eyes and laugh. "You're so stupid."

"Probably. Okay, definitely. Especially when it comes to you. You make me cray cray."

A raw laugh bursts from my throat. I slap my hands over my mouth and turn to look at him. I start cracking up when I see the grin on his face. "Making you laugh is way too easy. Really, Avery. Class things up a little bit." I continue to giggle and lean into him. "So, what are the odds that I get to keep you after this is over?"

I smile at him. I want to say yes, but I can't. Not yet. Not to mention that I never thought I'd find someone this way. "I don't know, Sean. What do we say when people ask how we met?"

"We tell them the truth—that we met on Deer Park Avenue when some jackass stole your car. No one needs to know anything else."

"Aren't you afraid they'll find out?"

Sean gives me a strange look. "Who? The press? My Mom? Who are we talking about, Avery? It's not like buying a hooker will ruin my reputation."

The smile slips off my face. "There's a fine line between fact and fiction. Don't you wonder what side you're asking that question from? I did things that I can't undo. No matter what you do, you'll never be the person who was bought and sold because she was broke. No one will condone that, like ever."

"We don't need anyone to condone anything, Avery. If you want to be with me, be with me." I look up into his dazzling blue eyes.

"I wish it was that simple."

"It is."

"No, it isn't. I need this job, but I don't want it. I need money to live, but—"

"I'll give you that—"

"But what does that make me, Sean? I go from being your hooker to being your—what—private call girl? I take money from you instead of Black? It doesn't feel right." It feels wrong. I glance out the window. I want a real relationship. I'm greedy, but I want things the way I want them. I want to work in an office and be able to pay my bills. I want to be able to go out on a date with Sean and not have to worry about whether or not I need to fuck the guy sitting next to us the following day. I want normal so badly, but my life is everything but normal.

"Avery…" Sean's voice trails off before he says anything else. I look up and see why. Gabe is standing outside my door with a garment bag. He knocks, and opens the door.

"Miss Stanz, your coat." He unzips the bag and takes the jacket off the hanger.

I smile when I see what he chose. It's a bright blue ski jacket with a purple reflective stripe across the shoulders and down the arms. He holds it out and I slip into it. "It fits." And it feels nice. I pull up the collar and snuggle into it. Damn it's soft. I glance down at the price tag and my eyes bug out of my head. "I can't wear this! It cost more than my car!"

"Mr. Ferro bought it. Yell at him." Gabe leans in to say something, but thinks better of it. He takes the door handle and gestures for me to move inside.

After I sit next to Sean and Gabe closes the door, I smack Sean in the chest with the palms of my hands. "You bought me a $1200 coat? What the hell, Ferro?"

Sean laughs and shoves me back. Gabe makes a noise in the back of his throat, like a warning. Sean ignores him. "Yes, I told him to get you something that was so soft and purple that you couldn't resist. It's more blue than purple, though. You might want to get your eyes checked old man." Sean glances at Gabe. Gabe holds the steering wheel tighter and grits his teeth.

I smack Sean's arm, so he stops taunting Gabe. "Sean, you can't buy me stuff like this."

"But I want to."

"But you can't. It's too much. You fixed my car and I didn't say anything, but this—"

"Is hardly enough. I know. I'll buy you more stuff."

"Sean," I warn.

"Avery." He smiles back at me. He's loving this.

I let out a rush of air and look at him out of the corner of my eye. "Arguing with you is pointless, isn't it?" He nods. "You know I won't wear it, right? I'll still walk around most days with no jacket at all."

"I understand." He's still smiling. He's still wearing that smug grin.

"So this is a waste of money…"

"Nothing is a waste on you. Stop fussing and just say thank you."

"No." I pout and fold my arms over the chest of my puffy coat. I can't find my boobs under this thing. I smack it down, trying to figure out where my folded arms should go.

Sean arches an eyebrow at me. "No? Did you tell me no?" He smiles and leans into me, pinning me to the seat with his body, as his hands find their way under my clothes to my skin—then he tickles me. His fingers move the perfect amount. It makes me wriggle and screech. I think Gabe is going to kill us when I slide off the seat and onto the floor, but he doesn't say anything. In fact, he puts up the divider.

Sean pulls me back up onto the seat and slips his hand under the jacket and then under my shirt. His eyes are locked with mine as his hand slides up along my waist to my side. He slows as he nears the bottom of my breast and brushes bare skin. Sean's eyes widen. "Where's your bra, Miss Smith?"

"I don't really know, Mr. Jones. I couldn't find it this morning, so I didn't wear one."

A look of pure lust flashes in his eyes. It makes me squirm in my seat. His hand slips to the button on my jeans. "What about these?" His eyes flick to my waist and then lower. He wants to know if I'm wearing panties.

"What about them?"

"Are you wearing any?" Sean watches me, waiting for a response.

I give him a lopsided smile and say, "Why don't you find out?"

Sean glances at the window and sees we have a ways to go. He leans into me, and slips the button through the hole. My jeans loosen and Sean presses his hand against my belly. His gaze is on mine, watching me, as his hand moves lower and lower. When he touches the V at the top of my legs, I close my eyes. Sean doesn't ask. He just does it. His fingers slip between the delicate folds and inside of me. His hand works slowly, teasing me, moving in circles until I'm saying naughty things in his ear.

Sean kisses my neck as he works his magic. My body responds to him instantly. Every touch sends me higher and higher. I tilt my head back and close my eyes as I push my hips to his hand. I want him to push me over the edge. I want to feel the tight coils within me unwind, but Sean keeps me there, right at the cusp.

It goes on like that. Sean teases me, touching me in all the right places until I'm gasping, begging for release. I moan his name and beg him, but Sean only smiles. Just when I think that I can't stand it for another second, he adds another finger and pushes into me—hard. I gasp and lift my hips to his hand. He thrusts harder and faster, rubbing my clit while he does it. I feel his eyes on my face, watching me. I'm suddenly very aware of the car and that we've stopped moving, but I don't care. My hips buck into his hand, and I cry out. The sensations shoot through my stomach and into my chest. I want his hands on me, in me. I'd do anything to come right now.

Frantically, I grab his shirt and pull Sean to my face. "Please…"

"Please, what? Tell me what you want, baby." His hand stills. His breath washes across my face. He smells so good and I want him so badly.

"Make me come. Please, Sean."

He grins. Sean's touch changes and sends a surge of lust shooting through my veins. I throw my head back and cry out. My hips slam into his hand and he pushes deeper inside of me. He does it over and over again, faster and harder. I wish my jeans weren't so tight. I wish we were naked and my legs were wrapped around his waist. I've never wanted to be fucked so much in my life. I have no idea what he's doing, but it feels so good.

Sean takes me higher and higher. My body tenses around his fingers, wanting release. Sean's rocking becomes rhythmic. He pushes faster and faster until I can't see. White blurs my vision. I try to keep my eyes open, but I can't. My hand clutches my breast as I scream his name. Sean pushes once more, hard, and holds. When he does that, the pulsing starts. He thrusts again and again as I come. I'm breathing so hard. My body stays rigid as ecstasy consumes me.

Sean keeps his hand between my legs until I open my eyes. Then he pulls out slowly and lifts my hand to his lips. He sucks on each finger, one at a time. "You are absolutely delicious."

I watch him through lowered lashes. Sean leans in and presses the pad of his finger to my lips. His hand has my scent. It hits me hard and makes me shy away, but Sean won't let me. "Open."

I do as he says and he puts a finger in my mouth—one he didn't lick clean. I close my eyes and suck. Sean leans in to me and takes his hand away. "Did you like that?" I nod slowly. I feel like I'm floating. I blink a few times and look out the window. We're at the park. Sean asks, "Are you ready?"

I nod slowly. Before Sean moves to open the door, I stop him. "Wait." I pull his lips down to mine and kiss him slowly and softly, until I'm so sated that I can't stop smiling.

CHAPTER 8

The snow is mixed with ice. It crackles under our feet. Gabe pulls the sled out of the trunk and mentions something about how easy a body would fit back there when he hands it to Sean. Gabe scares me when he sounds like that, because he isn't joking. The old guy nods at me as if he's doing me a service and then slips back into the car where it's warm.

I'm standing in front of Sean with my jacket open. The parking lot is a sheet of ice.

It hasn't been plowed yet. I'm grinning like a lunatic, ready to run across the parking lot and up the hill. There's a reason the locals call it Cardiac Hill—it'll give you a heart attack if you try to take it too fast. The thing is dauntingly steep, buy you can't really tell until you're on it. Runners go through these woods in the summer and come out into this clearing between the trees and the hill. It's a beautiful spot. I'm wondering how hard it's going to be to keep the sled from cracking into one of the towering pines.

Sean watches me for a moment, before taking the bottom of my coat in his hands and zipping it up to my neck. "You seriously need to get over that cold thing."

I raise an eyebrow at him. "You seriously need to get over that domination thing."

"It's not domination." He looks offended.

"Oh? Then what it is?"

"Control, that's all. Totally different." Sean glances at the snow covered hill.

"Yeah, in crazyland," I mutter and start walking, tugging the sleds behind me. Gabe couldn't shove a toboggan in the trunk, so we have a couple of plastic disc sleds. Gabe bought them on the way to pick us up, per Black's instructions. I wonder what Gabe's deal is, if he's here to protect me or what. I kind of think that he'll beat the shit out of me if Black tells him to. That part worries me. If I decide to stay with Sean, I have to repay her all the money I earned. That hardly seems fair, but then again, this isn't a job that I can quit. I brush the worry aside when I see Sean's face. His eyes are too big and his jaw is hanging open. "What?"

"Don't what me—I'm not into that kinky shit. I just like things a certain way."

It's almost laughable. Sean has no idea how far into kinky he's strayed. He left kinky behind a few states ago. "Ah, I see."

Sean walks up the hill with me as we talk. I try to carry the sleds, but Sean takes them from me. "You see what?"

"Denial with flashing neon signs. You really can't tell?"

Sean shakes his head and then looks at me, like he can't believe I'd say something like that. "I never thought of it that way. I mean, I don't do the whole dom/ sub thing. You really think that's what I'm doing?" I nod. He's quiet. I see the thoughts processing inside his head. His eyes are vacant and he's touching his face. His lips move silently, trying to reason it out. Finally, he shakes his head and says, "Holy shit, that's fucked up."

He believes me now. I take Sean's hand and start ticking things off. "You want control, complete trust, domination, submission—" Sean jerks his hand away. He looks annoyed. "I'm sorry, Sean. I thought you knew. It's nothing to be ashamed of. You like what you like, even if it is a little twisted."

Sean grumbles. I bump into his shoulder, but he doesn't smile. "I used to be..." he sighs, and pushes his hair out of his face. White bits of snow are clinging to his dark locks. Stubble lines his cheeks like always. "Different. Careful, you know. Now it's almost like I have to be a fucking predator to feel that way."

"What way?" When reach the top of the hill, we're both gasping for air.

Sean turns and looks at me. "I don't know, like I'm still alive. I'm numb all the time, Avery. Before I met you, I barely felt anything anymore. Having sex like that brings me back, but it doesn't last very long. Then, I need more. It's like a drug. The more I have, the more I want." He stares into space, lost in thought.

"Do you have something planned for later?" He nods. His icy eyes hold mine for a moment. "Is it like last night?"

"No, it's more intense. I didn't hold back last night, but I don't usually have sex with the same woman twice. It changes things. I need that raw emotion, but…"

"But what?" The sleds are on the ground. Sean put them down when we reached the top of the hill. There's a pink disc for me and a blue one for him.

I don't know what Sean means, or what he wants to do to me later. I'm not sure if I can tolerate more. Last night was a different kind of hell for me. I can't imagine enjoying that. Nerves flutter through me just thinking about it. More intense. Damn.

Sean beaks the silence. "I wish you liked it. I know you don't, so it makes me rethink things."

Smiling, I shake my head and exhale slowly. My breath makes a white cloud in the crisp air. "We're a pair of idiots. You know that, right? I mean, I want you to freely give yourself to me, and you practically want to rape me and whatever brains I have left."

Sean steps toward me. "You think that I'd rape you?" I just stare at him. I haven't the words or the heart to answer that question. Doesn't he realize what he's doing? That his fantasy is playing on a primal fear of being overpowered and sexually abused. It lurks at the back of mind all the time. I blink hard and look away. "Avery—"

"Sean, you need to look in the mirror and see the man you've become. I don't know who you were before, but the guy standing next to me is broken and dark. He comes to life when I'm terrified. He thrives at those times."

"I need it, Avery."

"You need something that I can't give you forever. If you don't bear your soul to someone, soon, this will get worse. You'll lose whatever piece of you that's left. You're hiding something dark, Sean, and it's eating you alive. I see it in your eyes. It weighs on your shoulders and crushes you until you can barely stand." I touch Sean's hand. It's so cold. He swallows hard and pulls out his gloves. "Don't you want to feel alive again? Don't you want to feel love and be loved?"

"I honestly don't know if I can. Things are so far gone. I'm..." he shakes his head and stops talking. I feel so bad that I tanked his mood like this. At least he's talking. I get the idea that Sean has a lot he needs to talk about, but no one he trusts enough to do it. He's stuck, reliving the same nightmare day after day.

I steer the day back to where it needs to go. Sean needs this too, he just doesn't know it yet. "You're going sledding, now. You're going to laugh, and scream like a girl. I'm going to make sure of that."

Sean gives me a weak smile. He doesn't believe me. Sean takes the disc and sits down. Before I climb on mine, I give his shoulders a hard push. Sean disappears over the side of the hill. I watch him try to control the disc as it curves down the incline. He laughs loudly as he grabs at the snow with his gloves trying to stop.

At the bottom of the hill, Sean jumps off the sled and looks up at me. "You suck, Smith!"

I grin. Today is going to be fun.

CHAPTER 9

When Sean finally reaches the top of the hill again, he runs straight at me and drops the sled. I squeal and try to get away, but the snow is too deep and my legs are too short. "That wasn't nice, Smitty."

I giggle and look over my shoulder just as Sean swipes his hand by my waist. He almost got me. I twist out of his reach and bounce around in the snow like a labradoodle, not moving very far, but avoiding his reach at the same time. "But it was very funny, Jones!"

"You're going to get punished for that."

"You have to catch me first." I'm grinning so hard that my face hurts. I make a bee line past him and jump on my sled. The disc does a one-eighty and I fly down the hill backward. I dig my hand into the snow on one side and whip the thing around. For once, I have good timing. A tree tried to hug my face, but I narrowly dodged it. One disaster avoided.

Sean shouts from behind me. He's on the other disc, coming down the hill behind me. He's laughing, smiling so widely that I get a flash of his dazzling grin when I glance back at him. "Oh, I plan on it!" He hits a bump and his last word is garbled with an *oof* sound when his disc smacks back down. Sean grips the side of the disc hard.

I start cracking up and don't notice the drop in front of me. The disc jets down into a ditch at the foot of the hill. The sled ends up perpendicular to the ground and plants itself like a headstone after throwing me off. I roll on my side several times, and then slide. It seems like forever. I'm almost in the parking lot by the time I skid to a stop. My hair is tangled around my face, forming a brown shroud. I lay there for a second trying to catch my breath while laughter starts building in my belly.

Suddenly, Sean is over me. "Avery, are you all right? Say something." He frantically brushes my long hair away from my face, trying to see if I'm hurt.

I sit up, laughing. My hair falls to my shoulders and down my back. It's covered in snow. "I suck at sledding."

Sean grins like he's trying not to laugh. He sits next to me in the snow. Sean can't keep a straight face. "That's a bit of an understatement. I think your sled hates you." Giggles rip through me until I can't hold them inside. Soon I'm laugh-snorting and can barely sit up. I laugh louder and longer, holding onto my stomach so it doesn't explode.

Sean laughs with me. The sound is so miraculous. It's rich and pure. He's happy in these moments. There's nothing bearing down on him, nothing tearing him to shreds. Sean flops back and lays next to me on the snow.

When the giggles fade away, I'm staring at the sky. It's gray. Little bits of snow continue to fall, but they're smaller now. It's getting colder.

"I worry about you, you know." Sean is looking at me. I turn my face toward him, not really getting what he's thinking. "This thing you have with the cold, it's…" he sighs and his words disappear.

"It's what?" I bristle a little bit. It's my one crazy flaw, well that and talking to my parents, but I need it. I'll defend what I do, how I cope.

Like Sean does. Damn it. I grit my teeth. Coping is coping.

A bunch of other thoughts run thought my mind, but Sean cuts them off when he scoots closer. He pushes up on his elbow and is over me. He pulls off a glove and strokes my frozen cheek while looking into my eyes. "It scares me, because it's too much like me. I don't want you to be numb, Avery. It's a shitty life, never feeling anything. And once you detach yourself that way, you can't ever come back. You worry me because it seems like you're still attracted to the idea."

Sean's hand feels so good on my cheek. I close my eyes and lean into his touch. The cold penetrated my clothing and the shivering has stopped. This is the point where sane people would go inside and warm up, but not me. I love feeling like this. I like it when the numbness turns to pain. I know what to do with that. I know how to react.

I press my lips together and watch the concern in his eyes. "I am attracted to the idea," I admit. "At least a little. But it's not just the numbness—it's the pain." My heart is racing. The way he looks at me could boil the snow in a flash.

Sean leans down to within an inch of my lips. He watches me through lowered lashes. His gaze flicks to my lips and then back to my eyes. "There are safer ways to make you feel pain."

My stomach twists. I want him to kiss me. He's so close, but he doesn't move. "Like in bed with you, Mr. Jones?"

"That's one way, yes. Think about it. It's safer than this. You're going to end up with frostbite or hypothermia." Sean stops speaking, but continues to look at my lips.

"Got something else to say, Jones?"

"No, nothing else to say at all." He closes the space between us and a rush of electricity shoots through my body. Sean has me so charged, so on edge, that when he touches me I'm ready to fly away. When his lips press into mine, I can feel his warmth and for once it feels better than the cold.

The kiss is gentle, careful. He licks the seam of my lips and I open. His tongue dances with mine as butterflies erupt inside of me. They flutter through my entire body until I flare back to life. My back is freezing and my front is warm because Sean is laying on top of me. One of his knees is between my legs. I push my hips against his as the kiss deepens. We're getting covered in snowflakes as we lay there, barely moving.

Sean pulls away breathless. "Come on. We can't drive all the way out here and only go down the hill once." He stands and brushes the snow off his jeans.

"Twice," I correct, and get up. I'm sweeping the snow off, not paying attention as I smile. "Well, you went down twice."

Grinning a wicked smile, Sean looks over at me. "I forgot about that. I owe you a punishment." The way he says it makes my stomach dip. I stop what I'm doing. I'm caught in his gaze, like it's a snare. He steps toward me and I swallow hard. Sean's hands slip around my waist and he slams my body into his hips. "Do you want it now or later?"

What the hell is he talking about? I thought he was kidding. From looking into his eyes, I know he isn't. I laugh, nervously, "Punish me? You need to take yourself a little less seriously."

"I'm sorry, what was that?" He cups his ear like an old guy and leans in closer to my mouth. "Did you say you want your punishment now?"

"No!" I laugh and back away from him.

"I think that's what you said. It was something like *Sean, I'm a really bad girl and I want it right now.*" The way he says it combined with the look in his eye makes my toes curl. Why does he seem hotter when he's acting twisted?

I have up my hand and I'm backing away from him with a huge smile on my face. "I think you heard me wrong, old man."

Sean's jaw drops for a half a second, then he rushes at me. His shoulder slams into me and we fall to the ground. My back hits the ground, but Sean cradles my head. Half a beat later, he's sitting on my chest and has my arms pinned above my head. "Old man," he mocks. "You really know how to turn a guy on."

I laugh and try to twist away. When that doesn't work, I say, "I want my punishment later. Later!"

Sean laughs and shakes his head. His dark hair is damp from the snow. "Oh, I don't think so. Let's see, what would be fitting for scaring the life out of me and pushing me down the hill?"

"What? Why am I getting two punishments?"

"It should be three—you ran away, too." Sean let's go of one of my arms and tries to hold me with his knee. I can dip my wrist backward, so I do it. I grab a fistful of snow and hurl it at his face. He gives me an incredulous look. "You did not just do that."

Before I can say anything, Sean flips me over, yanks down the back of my pants and spanks me three times. I yelp and try to get away, but his grip is too good. When his hand strikes my skin, the cold makes it sting longer. After the last strike, Sean shoves his hand down the back of my pants and pulls away. It isn't until he releases me and I stagger to my feet that I realize what he did. I screech and jump up and down. He put a ton of snow in my panties. "Oh my God! You suck! You suck! You suck!" I dance around, swatting at my butt, trying to get the snow out.

Sean smiles and folds his arms over his chest, watching me. "You deserved it."

There's too much snow. The skin on my hiney is stinging. I fall on my back and try to sweep out the snow that hasn't melted. I get most of it out and grab a hand full of snow. I stand and walk directly toward Sean. "That was evil."

He's smiling. His hands go into a defensive position. "I wouldn't do that if I were you. You'll just end up getting pinned to the ground and force fed snow."

"I eat snow for breakfast." I meant it to sound all butch and scary, but it doesn't. Sean laughs out loud. His eyes close as his shoulders shake with laughter. He looks up at the sky and laughs harder. I hurl my snowball at him and it smacks into the side of his face. He stops laughing. His eyes narrow and he races toward me.

I dart up the hill with Sean on my heels. He chases me and brings one of the sleds with him. When Sean catches me, he's breathing hard. His arms feel so good. I lean against his chest. Sean stiffens at first and then seems to relax. He lets me hold onto him, even though I'm sure he wants to peel me off. I glance up at him and say it. I don't care how stupid it is. I know how I feel and that's all that matters right then. "I love you, Sean."

He holds me tighter and kisses the top of my head. "I love you, too."

CHAPTER 10

Sean and I duck in the car behind the tinted divider after he's frozen. I don't mind, but Sean insists we warm up. Sean produces the thermoses and we both have a hot drink. It's weird, but Sean is a different person when sex isn't involved. He smiles and doesn't guard his thoughts as much. It's like he's been trapped in a cage and suddenly broke free. Sean's laughter rings out and his teasing is light and playful. I love this version of him.

"What are you thinking about?" he asks, and then takes a sip of cocoa. It's insanely hot. The hotel gave it to us on the way out. It's really good.

"I'm wondering what it would be like to be with the Sean that I saw out there." I point to the hill. There are tracks from where we were sledding, and a few piles of snow where I crashed. I'm a sucky sledder, but I own it, so it's all good.

Sean's lips twist into an awkward smile. He looks over at me after a moment. "I honestly don't know. When I'm with you and we're doing stuff like that—sledding, flying a kite, having a snowball fight—I don't feel like myself. It's like I forget everything that's happened for a few seconds and I can breathe again. I can't hold onto that guy, Avery. He didn't show up until you came along—I mean, I haven't felt that way in a very long time."

"I know what you mean." I tuck my hair behind my ear. "If you had a choice, which guy would you want to be?"

"I don't think it's that simple. I can't just forget everything. That guy is a shadow of what I was. You can't see it, but I can.

When I'm with you and we're laughing like that, it doesn't bother me. But when night comes…" he shakes his head and doesn't finish speaking.

I know about night time. I know what happens to my mind when evening spills across the sky like a bottle of ink. The darkness looms over me, crushing me. Sometimes it's all I can do to get to morning. Every unbidden thought and worry creeps to the front of my mind when my head hits the pillow. I try to shove them back down, but they don't stay. Dark thoughts start rolling through my mind and hopelessness chokes me until I pass out. Then, the next day comes and the cycle starts over again.

I touch his knee. Sean looks over at me. "I know. Believe me, I know what you're talking about."

Sean's phone beeps. He pulls it out of his pocket and looks at the screen. "It's getting late. Pete is almost to the city. We better head back."

I nod, and smile sadly. I lean into his arm and hold on tight. "Try to hold on to the feeling inside your chest. Hold it as long as possible. I know you're still in there, even if you don't. I see it, Sean. Don't give up. Not yet."

He wraps his arms around me and kisses my temple. "You think that we can pull each other up?"

I don't know. I want to say yes, but everyone thinks Sean is going down in flames. I shove aside their thoughts. They don't know him the way I do. They haven't lived my life. "Yes, because people like us already hit the bottom. Up is the only direction left to go."

CHAPTER 11

Gabe drops us off at the hotel. Sean and I have enough time to change before heading down to the restaurant. I take my time, putting on my make-up and doing my hair. Odds are that Gabe is going to report back to Black. I need to look perfect tonight so she doesn't strangle me tomorrow. I swipe on a final coat of mascara and pull out my thigh highs. The lace top on the stockings is so soft and pretty. I fasten them to the garters, then stand and smooth my dress. My hair is loose, hanging over my shoulders in soft waves. I had to put a vat of product in to make it look like that. My make-up turned out better than usual. I have smoky eyes and pale pink lips. They look kissable in this violet dress. It's silk—per Blacks instructions—with a narrow waist and a scoop neck. The skirt is fitted through the hip and then flares slightly. It showcases my features well. Marty would be proud.

Marty.

My mood darkens. I don't know what to do with him. Every time I check my phone, there are more messages from him, but I can't listen to them. What am I supposed to say? He tricked me. I feel like a moron. Sean kept telling me that Marty had a thing for me, but I didn't listen. I never saw it.

There's a knock on the bathroom door. "It's almost time to head down."

I shove aside my thoughts and walk to the door. When I pull it open, I look up at Sean. My god, he looks amazing. He's wearing a black suit that's cut perfectly to accentuate his frame. There's no tie around his neck though. Instead, the top button is open. His shirt is shade of charcoal, which makes his eyes look like sapphires. My breath catches in my throat.

While I'm looking him over, Sean's gaze travels up and down my body. A wicked smile stretches across his lips. "You look delicious, completely edible, Miss Smith."

I look away and feel my face flame red. It surprises me. After everything we've done, how am I blushing?

Sean reaches for me. He places his finger under my chin and tilts my face up. "You are amazing. Have I told you that?" I nod, smiling softly. "I think you need to hear it again. You are an amazing woman, Avery Stanz." He leans in and brushes his lips across my cheek. The touch is so light that my stomach erupts into flutters. "I love you."

I can't stop smiling. Everything is perfect. The thought of saying the L-bomb was something that always freaked me out, but it doesn't anymore. I like saying it to him. "I love you, too."

Sean pulls me to his chest and we stand there, just holding each other. His breath washes across my cheek and I hear his heart pounding in his chest. This frightens him? But he holds me anyway. I borrow his question and ask him. "What are you thinking?"

"I'm thinking that I should tell you what happened." His words hit me like a Mac truck. I look up at him and step back.

"Sean, you don't have to—"

Sean presses his finger to my lips and silences me. "I do, because it's not what they think. You were right about the papers. They don't know what happened. No one does." Tension flows over his body in sheets. Every muscle is corded tight. His gaze breaks away from mine and Sean starts pacing. He runs his hands through his dark hair and down his neck. He takes a deep breath and continues, "I never confessed to killing her, but everyone thought it was me. It was my gun. We were fighting before it happened. Everyone knew she was unhappy," he laughs, but it sounds miserable, "Well, everyone but me.

"Amanda called me that day. She asked me to come home. She said she didn't feel right, but when I pressed her she couldn't tell me what was wrong. I thought she was lonely. I told her that I was in the middle of a business transaction and couldn't leave—that I'd be home soon. My life was all business at that point, more so than now. Amanda understood that in the beginning. I loved her. I wanted to spend time with her, but I never got the chance. Then, everything changed."

Sean turns around and looks at me. He swallows hard, like he can barely breathe. "When I got home from work that night, I found her. She'd taken my gun and…" His voice catches as he shivers. Sean presses his lips together as I watch the horror play out on his face. "She shot herself. I didn't want her to be remembered like that. No one knew. Amanda kept everything inside. She always wore that polite smile and told everyone she was fine, happy even. That phone call was the only time she asked for help and I didn't give it to her." By the time he stops talking, Sean's eyes are glassy.

There are tears that want to fall, but he holds them back.

My eyes are so wide. "So you let them think you did it?" He nods and looks away. Oh my god. I'm trembling and that wasn't even my story. The pain in his voice is fresh, like it just happened. He's walked around with this secret for years, allowing it to devour him. The guilt he feels is etched across his face. Sean inhales deeply.

I walk up behind him. I want to touch him, to pull him into my arms, but he's paper-thin right now and that will hurt him more. I speak to his back. "No one knows you. The people who say you're calloused have no idea what they're talking about. Sean, look at me." When he doesn't move, I take his arm gently and turn him toward me. His lashes are clumped together, wet from tears that I didn't see fall. "It wasn't your fault."

"It was completely my fault. If I went home, if I—"

"You can't live that way. You can't question every decision you make. Constantly asking *what if* will make you crazy. You didn't know she was that far gone. You didn't know. This was beyond your control." *Awh fuck.* There it is. This is where that dark side of him is stemming from. This is the pinpoint location—the landmine. I knew the darkness was from losing his wife and unborn child, but this clarifies everything. The guilt is destroying him. It's why everything he touches turns to ash—he can't accept that it wasn't his fault. He believes he killed her.

Sean sees the puzzle pieces snap together in my eyes. "You gave me something I desperately needed last night. Talking about that day makes it worse. I'd ditch my brother and stay here with you."

"Talking about it will eventually make it better."

Sean gives me a weird look. "That's something a shrink would say."

I'm not a shrink. I know enough not to press on this spot too much. The whole thing could blow up in my face and I don't want to hurt Sean more than I already have.

I counter, "It's something a friend would say. Sean, you can't hold everything inside. It's warping you, twisting you into someone else." I reach for his hand and thread our fingers together. "I know you need sex that way. I understand now. Take anything you need from me later. I want you to. Don't hold back. I want my Sean back. I want the guy with the beautiful smile and the contagious laughter, the one that you thought was gone. He's still there. If I have any chance of being with him, I'll take it."

Sean nods slowly. He runs his hand over the back of his neck and looks down at me. "I wish I could say no."

"I don't want you to."

"Avery, I can't promise what you'll get."

"I'll get you—the dark, the light, and the monster within." I smile at him. "You protected her all these years by sheltering her death. You made it so that her friends and family would only focus on her life, and they must hate you for it. You protected her after she was gone, at all cost. I adore that man, and he's still in here." I press my palm to his chest. Sean tenses, but he doesn't move. "You're a good man with a dark façade. Believe that, because it's the truth."

Sean takes my hand and lifts it to his lips. The kiss is soft and light. "I love you,

Avery. I can't lose you too. It feels like the harder I try to hold onto you, the faster you slip away. I'm so sorry I hurt you. I never meant to—"

"Shhh. You already apologized and I accepted."

Sean nods and takes a steadying breath. He blinks away the emotions in his eyes and says, "We better get down there or Pete will think that I'm not coming. Keep me from doing something stupid, okay?"

"I'll try."

CHAPTER 12

Sean's emotions are well contained by the time we are seated at our table. Pete isn't here yet. Sean orders us something from the bar. I sip my wine, wondering how it is that Sean and his brother don't talk, like at all.

"Do you guys fight a lot?"

He shakes his head and puts down his glass. "No, it's not like that. Pete just has his own shit to deal with and I have mine. It was more of a natural isolation. I don't think he did it on purpose either, but the guy did change his cell number. I tried to track him down for our Mom, when he first disappeared, but Pete didn't want to be found. That's why this is weird."

As Sean speaks, I see Gabe walk by and sit at the bar. *Shit*. Why is he watching me from so close? Gabe makes a subtle movement that tells me to come over. Sean doesn't see him, not yet. I don't want tonight to be harder than it already is on Sean, so I excuse myself.

"I'll be right back," I stand and take my purse and walk toward the ladies room. Gabe follows. We stand in the alcove to the restrooms.

Gabe hands me a note. "From Miss Black. It's directions about your meeting with Henry Thomas tomorrow. She didn't like the stunt you pulled today."

"What stunt?"

"Fine, I didn't like the shit he pulled today. Just read the note." Gabe points a pudgy finger at the letter. I open it up and read fast.

Miss Stanz,

I expect you to dress appropriately from now on. Ripped jeans and mammoth sweaters that conceal your figure should be burned. I'm docking your pay to make sure you learn this lesson, since telling you is obviously not enough.

Keep Mr. Ferro on the leash. Do not give him everything he wants. He is a commodity that I want to keep in play.

Mr. Thomas is expecting your full services tomorrow. I expect you to perform at your best, which is more than a tease. I know you haven't had sex with this client and you are to change that immediately. No more teasing. Our girls don't behave that way.

Correct your behavior or I will correct it for you.

Give this letter back to Gabe when yo*u're finished.*

-*B.*

Gabe's hand is out. I shove the note back into his fist. *Fuck.* I glance up at Gabe and ask, "What will happen if I quit?"

"You did not just ask me that." He takes the note and holds a lighter to the corner. It burns quickly. Gabe drops it in the water fountain before anyone sees. He lifts out the charred note and it crumbles to dust in his hand.

"I can't do what she's asking me to do."

"You should have thought of that before you got into bed with Black. She doesn't share. Do not piss her off. Finish your contracts before you even consider mentioning fewer hours. You can try to slip out of it slowly, but if Black thinks you're taking guys on the side, she won't let you walk away. And I know you have another contract tomorrow. There's no way out of that one. You signed, girlie. You have to show up or she'll skin you."

My heart is pounding. The threat sounds literal, but it can't be. Mel would have said something. "Fine. Don't tell her that I said anything."

He laughs, like I'm hysterical. "I already told you—I like you. You seem like a good kid. You should have run when you had the chance."

My stomach twists. Gabe starts to walk away. I rush up next to him and ask, "What happens if I walk away now? Like I just don't show up tomorrow?"

"You don't want to know, kid." Gabe continues to walk. I stop in my tracks, with my heart in my throat. I told Sean that I wouldn't leave him. Damn it. What do I do? I need to figure out how to get out of this.

I walk back to the table and sit down. I smile, but it's too weak. Sean notices. "What's wrong?"

"Nothing." He gives me a look. God his eyes are so blue. "Fine, something, but I can't talk about it here. I'll tell you later."

"Is it about work?"

I nod. "Yes, I—" My words die in my mouth. A man is walking toward us. He has a muscular build and a trim body. Dark hair falls into his blue eyes and there's a crooked grin on his lips. His stride is confident, but damaged. There's a woman with him. She has big brown eyes and a mess of curly dark hair. The man holds onto her hand as they approach. I incline my head toward them and Sean turns to see what I'm looking at.

"Well, look at that." Sean sounds surprised and stands. He holds out his hand.

The man stops next to Sean and shakes his hand before pulling Sean closer and placing an arm over his shoulder. He slaps Sean's back a few times. "Good to see you, Sean."

"Pete." Sean nods and wriggles out of the hug.

Pete laughs after looking over at me. My jaw is hanging open. "Does she always look like that?"

The closer Pete got, the clearer it becomes. They look like clones. "Are you twins?"

Pete smiles. He seems so laid-back, so opposite of Sean. "Nah, that's what people always think when they see the three of us together, well, they think triplets. Jonathan's the youngest, and this guy is older than me. I'm the messed-up middle child." Pete grins at me and then at Sean. The woman standing behind him is silent. Pete asks Sean, "Well, are you going to introduce me, or do I have to do it myself?"

Sean is so tense that it looks like his face will crack if he speaks. "Avery, this is Peter Ferro—my younger brother."

Pete reaches for my hand and shakes it. He smiles and looks nervously over at his brother, like Sean will disapprove. "Actually, I ditched the Ferro part. It's Dr. Peter Granz.   Nice   to   meet   you."

******

Dr. Peter Granz is the
main character in
~DAMAGED~

******

*****

THE ARRANGEMENT SERIES

*****

This story unfolds over the course of multiple short novels. Each one follows the continuing story of Avery Stanz and Sean Ferro.

To ensure you don't miss the next installment, text AWESOMEBOOKS to 22828 and you will get an email reminder on release day.

**MORE ROMANCE BOOKS BY
H.M. WARD**

DAMAGED

DAMAGED 2

STRIPPED

SCANDALOUS

SCANDALOUS 2

SECRETS

THE SECRET LIFE OF TRYSTAN
SCOTT

And more.

To see a full book list, please visit:

www.SexyAwesomeBooks.com/books.htm

CAN'T WAIT FOR H.M WARD'S NEXT STEAMY BOOK?

Let her know by leaving stars and
telling her what you liked about
THE ARRANGEMENT VOL. 7
in a review!

CPSIA information can be obtained
at www.ICGtesting.com
Printed in the USA
LVOW03s1439200318
570509LV00002B/464/P